CHRONICLES OF DUNHAVEN

THE BLOOD REVELATION

BOOK 2

DAMIAN ALMARAZ

This book is dedicated to my readers and all the vampire lovers in the world. Your passion and enthusiasm fuel my imagination and drive me to create stories that haunt the night.

CONTENTS

PROLOGUE

In the misty Highlands of Scotland, where ancient castles stand as sentinels against the passage of time, Castle Dunhaven continues to be a beacon of mystery and power. The secrets that lay dormant within its ancient walls have now been awakened, and a new era of darkness and light is about to begin.

The Harrington family, having faced unimaginable trials, stands on the brink of a new adventure. The truth about their lineage and the connection to the mysterious Alexander has revealed only a part of the grand story Dunhaven jealously guards. James, the young heir to the castle, has discovered that his destiny is intertwined with ancient forces and dark powers that threaten to engulf the world.

With the arrival of new allies and enemies, the battle for the soul of Dunhaven will intensify. The revelation of how Alexander became a vampire and the source of his heritage and powers will mark the beginning of a saga that will transcend generations. But amidst this struggle, an unexpected tragedy and a mysterious kidnapping will alter the course of destiny forever.

Chapter 1

THE ORIGIN OF ALEXANDER

The fire crackled softly in the great fireplace of the castle as Alexander stared into the flames with thoughtful eyes. Sitting next to him, James couldn't contain his curiosity.

"Alexander, how did you become what you are?" James asked, his voice full of anxiety and anticipation.

Alexander sighed, his piercing blue eyes reflecting a deep sadness. "Many centuries ago, before Dunhaven was built, I was a young knight in a distant land. My life changed forever when I found an ancient amulet belonging to a secret order of vampires."

James listened intently as Alexander continued. "The amulet granted me unimaginable powers, but it also condemned me to an eternal existence. My lineage comes from an ancient race of vampires known as the Nocturnals, whose thirst for power and control nearly destroyed the world in a past era."

The revelation left James speechless. He understood that Alexander carried the weight of centuries of history and darkness. But before he could ask more, a noise at the door interrupted their conversation.

The sound echoed in the vast hall, reverberating through the castle's stone walls. Alexander stood up with surprising agility, his vampiric senses on high alert. James felt a chill run down his spine as the door slowly opened, revealing Sarah and David, who had been listening quietly.

"We wanted to make sure everything was alright," Sarah said, her voice trembling slightly. "We heard a strange noise."

Alexander gestured for them to come closer. "There's nothing to worry about, we were just talking about the past." His words were reassuring, but his gaze revealed deep concern.

"I'm glad we're all here," Alexander continued. "There is much you need to know about this castle and about me. The secrets it holds are not just mine, but yours as well."

The Harringtons sat around the fire, their expressions a mix of curiosity and apprehension. Alexander began to narrate his story in more detail, transporting them to a time when magic and darkness ruled the land.

"Centuries ago, before wars and betrayals divided the kingdoms, there was an order of vampires known as the Nocturnals. They were powerful beings, feared and respected for their wisdom and strength. Their mission was to protect the arcane secrets that could alter the fate of humanity. My family, the Alarics, led this order."

Alexander's story was filled with tragedy and sacrifice. He described how the Nocturnals had been betrayed from within by those who sought to use their power for evil. The resulting wars nearly annihilated their race.

"It was during those dark times that I found the amulet," Alexander continued. "It was hidden in a cave sealed by ancient magic. The amulet chose me, granting me powers beyond comprehension but also cursing me with immortality. Since then, I have wandered the world, protecting the Nocturnals' legacy and fighting against those who seek to destroy it."

James was both fascinated and horrified. Alexander's life was a testament to suffering and loneliness, but also to unyielding resilience. "And the castle?" James finally asked.

"What does it have to do with all this?"

"Dunhaven is more than just a castle," Alexander explained. "It is one of the last bastions of ancient magic, a place where the powers of the Nocturnals still reside. Your family, the Harringtons, are connected to this place and its history in ways you do not yet understand."

The atmosphere in the hall grew denser, charged with expectations and fears. Alexander knew that what was to come would test them all in unimaginable ways. But he also knew that together, they could face any darkness destiny might throw at them.

Chapter 2

AN UNEXPECTED FRIEND

The next morning, while James explored the castle grounds, he found an unexpected surprise. A lost and frightened golden retriever puppy had taken refuge near one of the towers.

The day was cold and gray, with a dense fog that wrapped everything in a cloak of mystery. Determined to discover more about the castle and its secrets, James had ventured through the vast gardens. It was then that he heard a soft whimper, almost drowned out by the fog.

Following the sound, James came to a small abandoned cabin, its walls covered in moss and its windows broken. There, huddled in a corner, was the puppy. Its large, sad brown eyes looked at James with a mix of fear and hope.

James knelt down slowly, extending a hand towards the puppy. "Hello, little one. What are you doing here all alone?" The puppy, trembling with cold and fear, approached James, sniffing his hand before cautiously licking it.

"I'll take you home," James said with a smile. "I'll call you Max."

With Max in his arms, James returned to the castle. Sarah and David, seeing the puppy, shared a look of concern. "James, you know having a pet is a big responsibility," David said firmly but kindly.

"I know, Dad," James replied, gently petting Max. "I promise to take care of him."

Sarah smiled and nodded. "Alright, James. Max can stay, but you have to make sure he is well taken care of."

Max quickly became a beloved member of the Harrington family. His presence brought new energy to the castle, easing some of the tension that had been growing since their arrival. However, fate had dark plans for Max.

One night, while the family slept, Max escaped without anyone noticing. The full moon illuminated the castle grounds, casting eerie shadows. Max, curious by nature, ventured beyond the safe limits of the castle, attracted by a noise in the distance.

The next day, James woke up to find Max gravely

injured by a vehicle that had passed through the castle grounds. The sight of his wounded friend filled James with despair.

"Alexander! Help me!" James cried as he carried Max in his arms, running towards the main hall.

Alexander arrived immediately, his eyes filled with concern at Max's condition. Without hesitation, Alexander bit Max, transferring part of his immortal power to him. The puppy, now a vampire with the ability to fly and transform into a small bat, miraculously recovered.

James watched in awe as Max transformed, his wounds healing at an incredible speed. "Thank you, Alexander," he said, his voice trembling. "I don't know what I would have done without him."

Alexander placed a hand on James's shoulder. "Max is strong now, but we must be careful. This was no accident. The vehicle that hit Max belonged to a group of vampire hunters who have been following us."

The revelation left James frozen. "Why are they following us? What do they want?"

"They want us, James," Alexander replied. "They want to destroy everything we protect. But we won't let them. Together, we will face this threat and protect our home and our loved ones."

The Harrington family knew their fight was just beginning. With Max now by their side, more powerful than ever, they were ready to face the hunters and uncover the dark secrets lurking in the shadows of Castle Dunhaven.

Chapter 3

THE HIDDEN THREAT

The peace in Dunhaven was shaken by the revelation of the true nature of the hunters. They had been planning their revenge against Alexander and any of his allies for generations. Max's conversion was an unexpected twist, and now the hunters were more determined than ever to eliminate the vampire threat.

James, Sarah, David, and Alexander prepared for the inevitable confrontation. Max, with his new powers, became a fierce guardian of the castle, protecting the family from the hunters' furtive attacks.

The castle, once a safe haven, now seemed like a battlefield in waiting. Nights grew longer and filled with tension, every sound amplified by paranoia. Sarah and David took turns keeping watch, while James and Alexander devised plans to defend against the hunters.

One night, under the full moon's light, James and Alexander ventured outside the castle. The thick fog made visibility difficult, but both knew they had to stay alert. The hunters were experts in stealth and ambush.

"We need to find out who is behind this," Alexander said quietly as they cautiously advanced through the forest surrounding the castle. "We can't let them catch us off guard."

James nodded, his heart pounding. Though he was scared, he knew he had to be brave. "Do you think they have a leader? Someone organizing them?"

Alexander frowned. "I'm sure they do. Vampire hunters don't act without a purpose. We need to find their leader and stop him."

Just then, a dull noise sounded to their right. Both turned quickly, their senses heightened. Max, in his bat form, flew silently above them, keeping watch from the air.

"Watch out!" James shouted as a dark figure lunged at them from the shadows.

Alexander reacted instantly, blocking the attack with supernatural strength. The figure retreated, revealing a hunter dressed in a dark cloak, eyes filled with hatred. However, before they could interrogate him, the hunter vanished into the fog, leaving an ominous warning in the air.

"This is just the beginning," Alexander whispered, his voice filled with determination. "We won't rest until this threat is eliminated."

But amidst the tension, a tragedy struck the family. One night, James disappeared without a trace. Desperation gripped Sarah and David as they searched tirelessly for their son, but their efforts were in vain. They didn't know if James had been kidnapped by the hunters or by something even more sinister.

James's disappearance plunged the family into an even deeper darkness. Sarah cried every night, while David was consumed by his despair. Alexander, feeling responsible, vowed to find James and bring him back.

"We will find him, Sarah," Alexander said firmly one night as they watched the moon from the castle battlements. "No matter what it costs, no matter how long it takes. We will bring James back safely."

The search for James became a personal mission for everyone in Dunhaven. Max, in his bat form, patrolled the skies, searching for any sign of his friend. Lydia and Marcus, the family's new allies, also joined the search, using their magic and skills to track the hunters.

Days turned into weeks, and weeks into months. The tension increased with each passing day without news of James. But hope did not fade. They knew that as long as they kept the faith and stayed united, they would find James and defeat the hunters.

The fight for Dunhaven was far from over, and the Harrington family prepared to face the darkness with renewed determination. The true battle had just begun.

Chapter 4

THE LEGACY OF THE NOCTURNALS

With James missing, Alexander decided to reveal more about his dark past. He gathered Sarah and David in the castle's great hall and began to tell them about the Nocturnals.

The hall, illuminated by the soft light of torches, was imbued with a solemn atmosphere. The stone walls, covered in ancient tapestries, seemed to listen attentively to Alexander's story.

"The Nocturnals were not just an ancient race of vampires, but also guardians of arcane secrets and powers that could change the course of history. My lineage traces back to the leaders of the Nocturnals, who guarded the amulet I now carry."

Sarah and David listened intently, understanding that James's disappearance was tied to these secrets. They knew that to find their son, they would have to delve into the darkness and face Alexander's enemies.

"The Nocturnals were more than mere vampires," Alexander continued. "They were beings of great wisdom and power, dedicated to protecting the world's balance. However, their power attracted envy and hatred from those who sought to use it for their own ends."

He described how the Nocturnals had been betrayed from within by those who desired absolute power. The resulting wars nearly destroyed their race and left deep scars on history.

"It was during those dark times that I found the amulet," Alexander explained. "It was hidden in a cave sealed by ancient magic. The amulet chose me, granting me powers beyond comprehension but also cursing me with immortality. Since then, I have wandered the world, protecting the Nocturnals' legacy and fighting against those who seek to destroy it."

David frowned, trying to grasp the magnitude of what Alexander was saying. "And what does this have to do with us? Why is our family involved?"

"Your family, the Harringtons, are connected to this place and its history in ways you do not yet understand," Alexander replied. "Castle Dunhaven was built on the foundations of a Nocturnal fortress. Your ancestors were allies of the Nocturnals, committed to protecting their secrets."

The revelation left Sarah and David astonished. They understood that their connection to the castle and to Alexander was deeper than they had imagined. "What do we do now?" Sarah asked, her voice filled with determination.

"We must find James and protect the castle," Alexander said firmly. "The hunters know about the Nocturnals' legacy and will do everything possible to destroy it. But as long as we are together, we have a chance to fight."

Alexander's story strengthened the family's resolve. They knew their fight was just beginning, but they also knew that together, they could face any challenge. With new allies and renewed determination, they prepared to delve into the darkness and save James.

Chapter 5

NEW ALLIES

In their search for answers, the Harrington family and Alexander found new allies. The first was Lydia, a powerful witch who had been watching over Castle Dunhaven for centuries. With her knowledge of ancient magic, Lydia became a valuable friend and guide.

Lydia appeared one night, emerging from the shadows with supernatural grace. Her long, dark hair cascaded over her shoulders, and her green eyes shone with ancient wisdom. "I have been waiting for this moment," she said, her voice soft but powerful. "The castle called me, and I knew my help would be needed."

Alexander received her with respect, recognizing her power and knowledge. "Lydia, your arrival is timely. We are facing a threat we cannot defeat alone."

Lydia nodded, understanding the gravity of the situation. "The vampire hunters have been active for centuries, but their current leader is more dangerous than you imagine. Viktor is a man without scruples, willing to sacrifice everything to gain the power of the Nocturnals."

The second ally was Marcus, a renegade vampire hunter who had left his order upon discovering the truth about the Nocturnals and their intentions. Marcus harbored deep resentment against his former order and was determined to help the Harrington family unravel the mystery and save James.

Marcus appeared one afternoon, seeking refuge in the castle. His rough appearance and scars told the story of many battles. "I have seen what my order has done," he said in a gravelly voice. "I can no longer support their actions. I want to help stop them and save James."

Sarah and David, initially wary, saw in Marcus a valuable ally. His knowledge of the hunters and their tactics would be invaluable in the coming fight.

With Lydia and Marcus by their side, the Harrington family and Alexander felt more prepared to face the threat. They gathered in the castle's map room, planning their next moves.

"We must be strategic," Alexander said as he pointed to different locations on the map. "The hunters know our weaknesses, but we also have our strengths. Lydia, I will need your magic to create protective barriers around the castle."

Lydia nodded. "I have already started working on that. But we will need something more to face Viktor. There is an ancient artifact hidden in the nearby mountains. It is a crystal that amplifies magic and can help us defeat the hunters."

Marcus intervened. "I know the place. I can guide you there. But it will be dangerous. The hunters have set traps and guards along the way."

The determination in everyone's eyes was palpable. They knew they had no other choice. They had to find the crystal and use it to save James and protect the Nocturnals' legacy.

The quest for the crystal became an urgent mission. With each passing day, the tension grew and the threat from the hunters loomed larger. But with their new allies by their side, the Harrington family felt stronger and ready to face any challenge destiny might throw at them.

Chapter 6

THE VAMPIRE HUNT

The search for James led the group to a series of confrontations with the vampire hunters. Utilizing their combined skills, Alexander, Max, Lydia, and Marcus managed to repel the attacks and advance in their mission.

The days turned into a series of constant battles, each more dangerous than the last. The hunters, led by Viktor, proved to be formidable adversaries, using cunning tactics and dark magic to try to defeat Dunhaven's defenders.

During one of these confrontations, Alexander found himself face-to-face with his former mentor and leader of the hunters, Viktor. The encounter revealed the deep betrayal that had led Alexander to become a vampire and the true nature of the threat they faced.

The confrontation took place in an ancient cemetery, shrouded in the night's fog. The old, time-worn gravestones created a labyrinth of shadows and echoes of a forgotten past.

"Alexander," Viktor said, his voice resonating with a

mocking tone. "I didn't expect to see you here. I thought you were hiding somewhere, licking your wounds."

Alexander clenched his fists, feeling the anger and betrayal burn within him. "Viktor, you should never have betrayed the Nocturnals. We entrusted you with our legacy, and you destroyed it for your ambition."

Viktor smiled coldly. "Power is for those willing to take it. The Nocturnals were weak, bound by their ideals of balance and protection. I found a more effective path."

The ensuing battle was fierce. Alexander and Viktor fought with an intensity that shook the cemetery, their powers clashing in a blaze of dark and luminous energy. Lydia and Marcus, along with Max, joined the fight, facing the other hunters surrounding Viktor.

James, still a prisoner, watched from a hidden cell, his heart pounding. Though he was scared, the sight of his loved ones fighting for him gave him hope and determination.

"Don't give up, James!" Lydia shouted as she cast a spell against one of the hunters. "We're here to save you."

James gripped the bars of his cell, looking for a way to free himself. He knew he had to find a way to help, even from within. He looked around, searching for anything he could use as a tool.

Finally, after an exhausting battle, Alexander managed to disarm Viktor, leaving the hunter leader defenseless. "This ends now, Viktor. I will not let you destroy what remains of the Nocturnals."

Viktor, despite his defeat, smiled with unsettling malice. "This is just the beginning, Alexander. The true darkness has yet to awaken."

With those words, Viktor vanished in a cloud of smoke, leaving Alexander and the others with more questions than answers. Though they had won the battle, the war was far from over.

The group gathered around James, finally freeing him from his cell. "Thank you," James said with a trembling voice. "I knew you would come for me."

Alexander hugged him tightly. "We never leave anyone behind, James. We're in this together."

With James safe, the Harrington family and their allies returned to the castle, knowing they had made a significant breakthrough. But they also knew the fight was not over. They had to continue protecting the Nocturnals' legacy and prepare for any new threat that might arise.

Chapter 7

THE NOCTURNALS' REFUGE

Guided by the clues they had discovered, the group ventured into the ancient refuge of the Nocturnals. This place, hidden in the depths of a mountain, was filled with traps and dangers. However, it also contained crucial answers about James's whereabouts and the Nocturnals' secrets.

The journey to the refuge was arduous and dangerous. They crossed dense forests and turbulent rivers, facing magical creatures and ancient traps. Each step brought them closer to their destination, but also increased the risk of being discovered by the hunters.

Finally, they reached the entrance of the cave leading to the refuge. The entrance was hidden behind a waterfall, and only those with the proper knowledge could find it. Lydia used her magic to open the way, revealing a dark, narrow passage.

"This is the place," Lydia said, her voice echoing in the cave. "Here is where the Nocturnals kept their most valuable secrets."

The group advanced cautiously, their steps echoing in the cave's silence. The walls were covered in ancient inscriptions and magical symbols that told the story of the Nocturnals.

James, feeling a strange connection to the place, stopped in front of a particular inscription. "Alexander, what does this say?"

Alexander approached and read the inscription aloud. "It speaks of the amulet and its power. It says that only a direct descendant of the Harringtons can unlock its full potential."

The revelation left everyone silent. James, understanding the magnitude of his heritage, felt overwhelmed. "Does that mean I can use the amulet?"

"Yes," Alexander replied seriously. "But it also means you are in great danger. Viktor and his hunters want you for this reason. They want to use your power for their own ends."

The group continued to explore the cave, searching for the crystal Lydia had mentioned. After several hours of searching, they finally found it in a hidden chamber, illuminated by a magical light.

"This is the crystal," Lydia said reverently. "With this, we can amplify our magic and face Viktor with more strength."

As they prepared to leave the cave, a dark shadow moved on the periphery of their vision. Max, in his bat form, screeched a warning.

"We're surrounded," Marcus said, drawing his sword. "The hunters have found us."

The ensuing battle was intense and brutal. The hunters, led by Viktor, attacked with relentless fury. Alexander, Lydia, Marcus, and Max fought with all their power, protecting James and the crystal.

James, determined not to be a burden, used his newly discovered power to help in the fight. He channeled the amulet's energy, creating protective barriers and casting spells against the hunters.

Finally, after an exhausting battle, they managed to repel the hunters and escape the cave. Though they were wounded and tired, they knew they had achieved a significant victory. With the crystal in their possession, they had a real chance to defeat Viktor and protect the Nocturnals' legacy.

They returned to the castle, where they began to plan their next move. They knew the final battle was approaching, and they had to be prepared to face it with all their strength.

Chapter 8

THE RESCUE OF JAMES

Armed with this new information, the group devised a plan to rescue James. They knew time was running out, as the vampire hunters were determined to use James for their dark purposes.

The castle became a center of frantic activity as they prepared their assault. Lydia worked tirelessly to strengthen the magical defenses, while Marcus and Alexander planned the combat strategy. Max, now fully adapted to his new abilities, patrolled the grounds, ensuring there were no surprises.

"We must act quickly," Marcus said as they reviewed the map of the hunters' fortress. "We know Viktor plans to perform a ritual with James during the next full moon. If he succeeds, his powers will be amplified and he will be nearly impossible to stop."

"Then we have no time to waste," Alexander replied with determination. "We will attack tonight. With the crystal and our combined skills, we can defeat them."

The tension in the air was palpable as they prepared for the assault. Sarah and David, though worried, knew they had to trust Alexander and their allies. "Bring our son back," Sarah said with tears in her eyes. "Please, bring him back."

Under the cover of night, the group set out for the hunters' fortress. The full moon illuminated their path, casting long and sinister shadows on the ground.

The fortress was heavily guarded, with sentries patrolling the walls and magical traps protecting the entrances. But Alexander, Lydia, Marcus, and Max were prepared. They used their skills to evade the guards and disable the traps, advancing stealthily towards the heart of the fortress.

Inside the fortress, James was chained in a dark cell, his mind filled with fear and despair. He knew time was running out, and each moment that passed brought him closer to Viktor's ritual.

Suddenly, a familiar sound broke the silence. It was Max's screech, followed by the sound of a battle in the distance. James felt a surge of hope as he realized his friends had come for him.

"I'm here!" James shouted, his voice echoing in the cell. "Please, help me!"

Alexander and Marcus arrived first, breaking the chains that held James and pulling him out of the cell. "We're here, James. We're taking you home," Alexander said with a reassuring smile.

But before they could escape, Viktor appeared, his face contorted with anger and hatred. "Not so fast, Alexander. This boy is mine."

The final battle was intense and ruthless. Viktor used all his dark power to try to stop Alexander and the others, while James and Marcus fought to stay safe. Lydia, with the crystal in hand, channeled her magic to protect the group and attack Viktor with devastating force.

Finally, in a final act of sacrifice, Alexander used the amulet's power to unleash an explosion of energy that defeated Viktor and destroyed the hunters' fortress. The battle was over, but the cost had been high.

With Viktor defeated and James safe, the group returned to the castle, knowing they had achieved a great victory. But they also knew the fight was not over. They had to continue protecting the Nocturnals' legacy and prepare for any new threat that might arise.

Chapter 9

THE PRICE OF FREEDOM

Although they had rescued James, the cost had been high. Alexander was gravely wounded in the battle, and Lydia revealed that the amulet had a price: each use drained the life of its bearer.

The atmosphere in the castle was somber as everyone gathered around Alexander, who lay on a bed, his face pale and sweaty. Lydia was by his side, using her magic to try to heal the most serious wounds, but they knew the damage was deep.

"Alexander," James said with a trembling voice, "all of this is my fault. If it weren't for me, you wouldn't be like this."

Alexander opened his eyes and took James's hand. "It's not your fault, James. Everything I did, I did because I believed in you and what you represent. You are the key to protecting the Nocturnals' legacy. Never forget that."

The Harrington family and their allies knew they had to make a difficult decision. The amulet, though powerful, was a dangerous burden. They knew that to protect James and the castle, they would have to make sacrifices.

Sarah and David looked at each other with tear-filled eyes, understanding the gravity of the situation. "Alexander, is there any way to save you?" Sarah asked desperately.

Alexander shook his head, a sad smile on his lips. "The amulet has been my burden for centuries. I always knew this moment would come. But there is a way to protect James and the castle. I must use the amulet one last time to seal the dark powers of the Nocturnals and protect all of you."

The decision was difficult, but they knew they had no other choice. Guided by Lydia, Alexander prepared to perform the final ritual. Everyone gathered in the great hall, where the amulet glowed with an ethereal light.

"James, come closer," Alexander said softly. "You must witness this ritual. It is part of your legacy."

James approached, his heart pounding. He felt a mix of fear and determination, knowing he was about to witness something extraordinary.

Alexander began to recite ancient words in a forgotten language, his voice resonating with a power that filled the hall. The amulet glowed intensely, radiating a light that enveloped everyone.

Suddenly, an explosion of energy filled the hall, and Alexander was lifted into the air by an invisible force. His body glowed with a blinding light as the amulet absorbed the darkness and sealed the Nocturnals' powers.

With a final breath, Alexander slowly descended to the ground, his body still and serene. The amulet, now extinguished, fell from his hands, marking the end of the ritual.

James, with tears in his eyes, knelt beside Alexander, feeling deep sadness and gratitude. "Thank you, Alexander," he whispered. "I promise to protect the Nocturnals' legacy and make you proud."

The Harrington family and their allies joined in an embrace, knowing they had lost a great friend and protector, but also knowing that his sacrifice would not be in vain. The fight for Dunhaven would continue, and together, they would face any challenge the future might bring.

Chapter 10

THE FINAL BATTLE

The final battle against the vampire hunters was fierce and desperate. Alexander, with the help of Max and his allies, fought valiantly to protect the Harrington family and the legacy of Dunhaven.

At the climax of the battle, Alexander used the amulet to unleash a devastating power that destroyed the hunters and sealed the dark forces of the Nocturnals. However, this sacrifice cost him his life, and Alexander disappeared in a burst of light.

With peace finally restored, the Harrington family began to rebuild their lives. James, having learned about his lineage and powers, committed himself to protecting the legacy of Dunhaven and the secrets of the Nocturnals.

Max, now an immortal guardian of the castle, continued to watch over and protect the family. Lydia and Marcus stayed to help with the reconstruction and ensure that the dark forces would never again threaten the castle.

Castle Dunhaven, though marked by battles and

sacrifices, became a symbol of hope and resilience. The Harrington family, united by their experiences, prepared to face any challenge the future might bring.

And as the stars shone in the sky, illuminating the night with their gentle light, they knew that no matter where their journey took them, Castle Dunhaven would always be their home, a beacon of hope in a world full of darkness.

.

EPILOGUE: THE NEXT GENERATION

Years later, James, now an adult, became the guardian of Dunhaven's legacy. With the help of Lydia and Marcus, he continued to protect the castle and the secrets of the Nocturnals.

One day, while exploring the castle grounds, James found a lost and frightened boy, reminding him of his own childhood. He decided to take the boy in, giving him a home and teaching him about the legacy and responsibilities of being part of Dunhaven.

The story of Dunhaven continues, with new challenges and adventures awaiting on the horizon. But with the Harrington family at the helm, the castle and its secrets will be protected for future generations.

ABOUT THE AUTHOR

Damian Almaraz, a passionate storyteller with a love for the dark and mysterious, resides in the enchanting landscapes of Mexico with his partner of 12 years and their three beloved dogs, Estrella, Luna, and Brownie. With a profound fascination for vampire and werewolf novels, Damian immerses himself in the world of terror and the paranormal, weaving tales that captivate and thrill his readers. His deep understanding of the supernatural is evident in his writing, where every page is filled with suspense, intrigue, and the unknown. When he's not writing, Damian enjoys exploring haunted locations, seeking inspiration for his next spine-chilling adventure. His stories are a testament to his dedication to the genre, inviting readers to journey into realms where the supernatural reigns supreme.

ACKNOWLEDGMENTS

To my partner, thank you for being my constant source of inspiration and strength. Your unwavering support makes everything possible.

To my readers, your commitment to my first book and your willingness to follow me on this journey means the world to me. Without you, I am not who I am today.